The Story of Thumper
The Cleft-Affected Bunny

By Joanne Green

Illustrated by Penny Tennant

Publisher: Saga Books Press
www.sagabooks.net

Cover art by Penny Tennant
Cover design by Debra Shively Welch

ISBN: 978-1-897512-14-2

This book is dedicated to my son Joey, the little boy who "only needed a home," and grew to be an amazing kid!

JG

This book is dedicated to my children, Kate, Phillip and Andrew, also to Mr. Whiskers, the pet bunny I had as a child.

PT

The Story of Thumper, the Cleft-Affected Bunny

Preface:

The story of Thumper is true. Thumper was a real bunny who was born with a real cleft in his lip. The cleft was located on the right side, widening his natural rodent cleft and extending all the way up into and on top of his nose. He was passed over in favor of his littermates when the litter was sold as pets. He was eventually purchased at a bargain price for a little girl who did not want him. She did tease him and he did bite her, resulting in his return to the pet store. I received a phone call from my friend who was at the store looking for a rex for her own little girl. She was excited as she told me that there was a bunny at the story that was meant to be mine. I am the mother by adoption to three beautiful children – each, like Thumper, born with a cleft lip.

When I took my son, Joey, to the pet store with me, finding the bunny hidden away in a staff bathroom, my son knelt down on his knees and gathered the soft bunny into his arms. He looked up at me and said, "Mom. All he needs is a home." I reflected back ten years to the day my adoption agency presented to me a picture of a tiny child that had lived far too harshly through his first year of life. Many times his folder went out to prospective families, and every time, it came back – "No. We don't want a child with a severe bilateral cleft." I held that picture in my hand and I knew I was looking at my son. I turned to my husband and said, "But all he needs is a home. We have a home." How could I possibly turn down the very words echoed back to me from the very child who came home to the love we had for him?

Thumper has gone on to teach valuable lessons to others who were born with a difference. Unlike Thumper, when a child is born with a cleft lip, it is often repaired within the first few months of life. However, the resulting scar and sometimes the nasal-sounding speech can make a child feel just as different as Thumper was treated. Sometimes others cannot see the beauty of the person behind the scar, and that can hurt deeply. Thumper's lesson is that nobody has to change to be loved and accepted. They only need to be understood.

Thumper remained a dearly loved pet in my home for a number of years. One day he picked up a respiratory infection and the next day, he died. It was a sad day in my home as we mourned the passing of a pet and a friend. I am comforted to know that he lived many happy years and died contented and loved. Yet, his legacy lives on. Thumper continues to share his life with children everywhere through the pages of this book.

One thing we can all learn from Thumper's life is this: Different cannot mean less.

ULTIMATE PROTECTION
by Joanne Green

I monitor the foods he eats,
That he will grow up strong.
I guide his moral development
By teaching right from wrong.
I dress him warm on colder days,
And of course we immunize.
I teach him rules of safety to
Ensure his choice is wise.

If only I could hold a shield
To turn all hurts away
I'd stand a martyr's vigilance
And protect him night and day!
But there comes a time when it no longer
Does him any good
That I continue to hold the shield
That he more appropriately should.

And that becomes especially true
When peer relations start;
When hurts don't hurt his body so much
As they truly hurt his heart.
I could protect him - hold the shield -
Turn slandering others away
Or I could pass the shield to him
To keep the darts at bay.

When comments hurt my little boy
I die a bit inside.
But when I see him face his pain
I understand with pride.

Ultimately the battle is his
And he will learn to deal
With ugly words and painful wounds
That he alone must heal.
I want always to protect him,
And I know I always will,
But the best way to protect him
Is to provide him with that skill.

One Spring morning, Thumper was born, along with seven brothers and sisters! What a crowd of bunnies they made! Momma Bunny looked over each of her new children. Four boys, four girls. Two boys were pure white. One girl had three black spots on her back, and two girls were white with brown spots. The last girl was all brown, just like her brother. And Thumper was white with black rings around each eye.

And Thumper was white with black rings around each eye.

But Thumper was different from his brothers and sisters. Thumper's lip and nose looked different. His face looked somehow, not quite finished. The skin on his lip didn't come together like it did for the other bunnies in the litter. Thumper's lip was cleft.

Momma Bunny looked Thumper over and thought, "Hmmm, This one will likely be weaker. Too bad. He really is pretty. Well, I must look after the strongest of my babies. Too bad about this one."

(Animals are like that, but people are not, you know.)

Thumper's brothers and sisters also thought Thumper looked weak and they were very mean to him. They often pushed him away from the food when they all began to eat. "He is too weak." they would say, "He should not eat our food. We will be strong, but this bunny will not. We must save the good food for ourselves and let him eat what we leave over."

(Animals can be like that, but people are not, you know.)

And so they pushed Thumper away from the food when it was time to eat, and when the other bunnies finished their meals, Thumper was allowed to eat only what was left. And soon, Thumper was different from his brothers and sisters in yet another way. He grew to be much smaller than the rest.

Those brothers and sisters played and had a good time between themselves. But they pushed Thumper away. "We do not want to play with you." They said. "You are weak, and you look different. We cannot be seen playing with a bunny that looks different." And so they pushed him away, and Thumper felt sad and lonely.

(Animals can be like that, but people should not, you know.)

Thumper dreamed of the day that a family would take him home from the litter to be their own bunny. He thought of warm hugs and gentle pettings and a hutch of his own with food of his own that he would not be pushed away from.

It was a wonderful dream.

Late that spring, one-by-one his brothers and sisters went home to families where they were loved and hugged.

An elderly woman claimed Dot for her grandchildren.

Snowflake joined a family who had three other bunnies already.

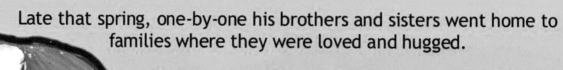

As the rest of the brothers and sisters found homes of their own, Thumper realized that nobody was going to choose him – the bunny with the different-looking lip.

Spotty went home with a red-headed little girl. Daphne and Thelma found a home together with twin boys.

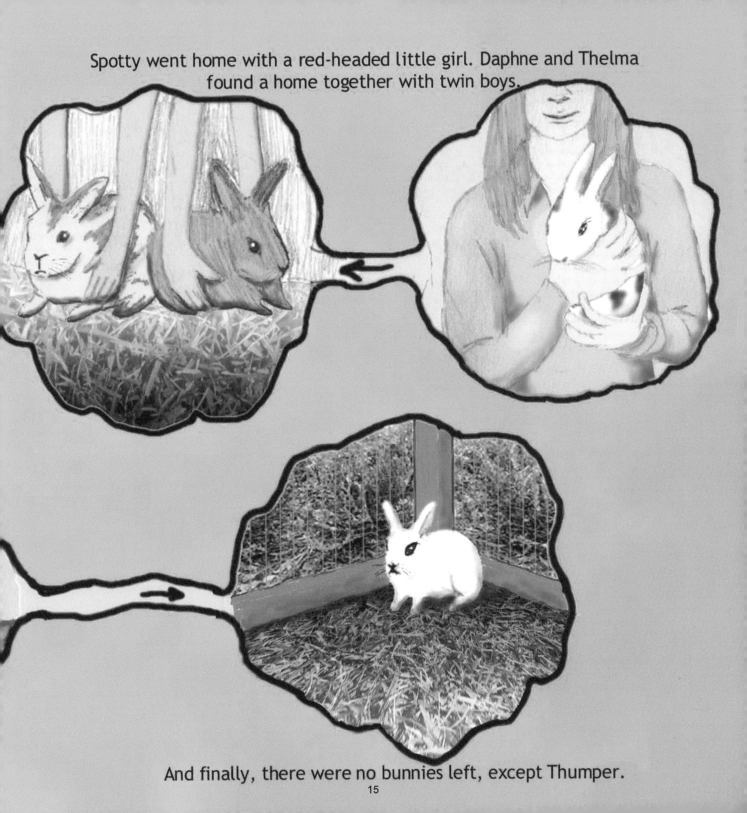

And finally, there were no bunnies left, except Thumper.

At last a family came in to buy a bunny. Thumper carefully cleaned his whiskers and polished his ears. He sat as straight and alert as he could, hoping that the last family would not notice his different-looking face.

But they did. They wanted a bunny so bad that they asked the breeder to sell them the last little bunny for half price because after all, his lip looked a little different. And so, at long last, Thumper went home. It was not the way he had dreamed of his homecoming, but he had his own home after all.

The little girl in the new home saw Thumper and cried. "Why did you buy me a rabbit with a broken face?" She did not like her new bunny. She would not hold him. She would not hug him. She put him in a cold cage and forgot him. Some days she did not even remember to feed him.

Thumper was lonelier than he had ever been. And he was angry, too. Animals had treated him badly, but people were supposed to be different! But these people were not different.
They still pushed him away and treated him badly. They would not play with him. They forgot him in his cage and left him all alone. And sometimes they teased him through the bars of the cage.

Thumper was angry and hurt and lonely and sad. And one day when the little girl pushed her fingers between the bars of the cage to tease him, Thumper bit her!

And that was the end of Thumper in THAT family. "Oh, the horrible rabbit!"
shouted the mother, as the little girl wailed and sobbed.
"That rabbit is mean! We cannot have him biting our child!"
And so off to the pet store he went.

The pet store people did not know what to do. Thumper still looked different, so they thought he would be difficult to sell. Thumper was tired of being treated badly by everyone, so he let all the other rabbits in the hutch know that he would not let them push him around.
The store people thought he was mean.

Customers came into the store and saw Thumper. Most of them made comments about Thumper's different-looking face, and they laughed at him. So the store people put him away where no one would see him, in the bathroom in the back. Thumper was very sad and very lonely. He was certain that life was hopeless.

But one of the customers was not laughing at Thumper. She knew just the family who would love to give him a home.

She raced home to call the family.
"Go to the pet store. There is a bunny there that is meant to be yours!"
she shouted.

The mom and her son drove to the pet store. When they went in they did not see a bunny that was 'meant to be theirs', so they asked,

"Do you have another bunny here? One with a different-looking lip?"

The store people took the mom and the boy to the bathroom where they were keeping Thumper.

When the mom saw the scared, lonely little bunny, she knew right away that the bunny was meant to be theirs. The boy, Joey, scooped the bunny into his arms and felt his soft fur. He gently pet the bunny and put his cheek right next to the bunny's own cheek, as a tear fell from the mom's eye. The boy looked up at the mom and said,

"Other people have been mean to him, Mom. He just needs us to love him."

The mom agreed. For they both knew how much Thumper needed to be loved by people who could love him just the way he was.

The mom's little boy, Joey, had also been born with a different-looking lip. And Joey was a terrific and loving little boy.

The mom and her son lovingly took the bunny home where they gave him everything he needed to be a healthy, happy bunny.

They gave him a comfortable hutch, plenty of food and water, toys to play with and lots and lots of love.

And slowly Thumper learned to trust his new family.

People could be like that. Thumper had always hoped that it could be true. And finally, at long last, for Thumper, it was.

Helps and Information for Children and Families

who deal with the issues related to Cleft

A Parent's Role in Defining a Cleft in the Life of Their Child

I think the most important time of the child's life is... well... all of it, basically. And at all times, parents can make the biggest contribution to the child's self-image.

As babies... love, love, LOVE that child.... unconditionally... thoroughly... ALL of the child. Kiss his little cleft and look him in the eyes and honestly tell him how incredibly beautiful he is and how much you love him. Don't hide him away, and don't "protect" him from the child that he is. Let your own attitude dictate the direction that the attitudes of others around him are going to take. He's not a tragedy, he's not a sorrow. He's your own precious baby, and a bundle of everything lovely.

As toddlers and pre-schoolers, lay the foundation of acceptance and understanding. Talk openly about the cleft. It's easy at that time. There's lots going on. Tell the birth story (or adoption story) time and again, and include the cleft in that story. Let him see his baby pictures, and explain it to him in terms he can understand. "See how it looked broken? It wasn't broken. It just didn't grow together before you were born. The doctor helped it grow together with an operation....." Let him know that this subject is never taboo in your house, and that there is nothing that cannot be discussed in your arms.

As school-aged kids... Be there to help, to educate his growing world, to listen, to comfort. There are many new experiences, and for the first time since he was born, he will be fielding the questions for himself. This is also the time that we let go of the cleft as a central focus in his life (one of several, to be sure) and realize on our own that if we did our jobs well, it finds a niche of perspective in our child's life too. Yes, there is the cleft, and he can answer the questions that may come his way... but there is also soccer, and baseball, and homework, and that neat field trip to the planetarium, and everything else that fills a young child's life - including lots and lots and lots of friends. This is also the time when enemies are formed, and bullies come out of the cracks of their own low self-esteem. If it happens, and your child is bullied, you are there to comfort him and empower him such that he can either stop the bullying or hold the shield that stops, or muffles, the hurt.

In their teens, we as parents are far from done. We are there to help our child deal with the angst of their budding independence, and to help them keep their physical selves (so important at this age) in perspective. The cleft is only one part of their lives, only one issue that they deal with. New surgeries coming at this age can make major or minor changes to the face they see in the mirror - NOT a good age to change a part of one's identity... but this is still the age for it for some.

He didn't get the part in the play (was it the cleft?) He didn't get elected for the student body office he ran for (was it the cleft?) The girl of his dreams is dating someone else (Is it the cleft?) No. It's life. Not every child gets the part in the play, not every candidate wins the election, not a single person gets through life without a broken heart at one point or another.   Convince him of his wonderfulness and goodness, and let him step back up to the plate and take another swing at life. Cleft or no cleft, the hormones rage at this point in life, the body changes, and emotions (particularly in girls, but boys do NOT escape it) go wild. It's the most fun time of a person's life, and the hardest too. Our babies are fledging and they are scared, and we are scared, but they (and we) have to get through this time of development, and we do. For some it is relatively painless. For others, it's a struggle the likes of which could not have been imagined. Cleft, or no cleft.

The tools we give our children have a tremendous impact on how well they handle their world. We parents cannot underestimate the value of our role in our children's lives as they travel this well-trodden road toward independent adulthood.

What an adventure!

TEN WAYS TO ENHANCE YOUR CHILD'S SELF-IMAGE

A person's self image is intimately related to self esteem. How one sees ones self (self image) determines how one feels about who he or she is (self esteem). As parents we want our child to have a healthy sense of self esteem. The best way to ensure that that happens, is to be concerned with his self image.

How do you ensure a healthy self image? Consider yourself, and every other person in your child's life, to be something of a "Hall of Mirrors" You know the place - some mirrors distort the image, some give true representations. Some enhance an image (for instance, some might make a short, heavy person appear tall and thin) and many make the image a comic representation of itself.

Every time your child sees himself through the eyes of someone else, he is looking into that person's mirror, and forming a self image based upon the image he sees. Therefore, if others see a child as "ugly", "stupid", "lazy", or "inferior", sooner or later that is how the child will see himself. If others instead reflect an image of "beautiful", "intelligent", "industrious", or "superior", then that is the way the child will identify himself.

But no two "mirrors" will reflect the same image. Peers may see a child differently than parents; teachers may have a different view than grandparents. The goal is to help your child form an inner mirror - the one by which he will measure all others, allowing him to reject the inaccurate images of himself.

The following are ten ways to enhance your child's self image through your home environment. These steps will help your child see himself as a positive and valuable person.

1. Do not allow your child's craniofacial condition to define him as an individual. My son has a cleft. But he also has bright, sparkling eyes, a winsome personality, an active imagination, and many more attributes. Some parents actually refer to their child as "a cleft". In reality, you have "a child", and your child has a cleft.

2. Love your child unconditionally. Do not allow your child to think that your love is dependent on anything he or she has done or can do. Do not let your child think that love is dependent upon personal beauty. If a child feels that your love is dependent on something, then losing that something can, in your child's mind, make you stop loving him or her.

3. Cultivate a home environment in which each person's worth as an individual is affirmed. Share feelings, experiences, etc. Enjoy life together as a whole family unit.

4. Help children to experience good feelings about themselves. Instead of saying, "I feel so proud of you for that." say, "Do you feel proud of yourself for that?" or "How does that make you feel?"

5. Provide a good example. Children must feel that it is not conceited to feel good about themselves. Let your child know that you, in fact, feel good about who you are. That gives him permission to feel good about who he is.

6. Cultivate friendships with many diverse people. Your child must be given the opportunity to experience the notion that there is not a very narrow focus of what is "acceptable". The people in your child's life should portray the rich diversity that is available to us in this big, wonderful world. In recognizing a wider band of what is "acceptable and positive", your child will be more likely to find himself within that band.

7. Be aware of and tone down your own attitudes based on "looks-ism". Do you often point out people who are "good looking", or who have flawless bodies? Do you make negative comments about persons who are not beautiful? Do you comment on the physical beauty of TV or movie personalities? Every time you do that in your child's presence, you are, in effect, saying to your child, "Physical perfection is all that matters in this world".

8. Always point out positive attributes about others that do not involve the physical. Rather than identifying people by race, hair color, height, weight, etc, try finding some other way to describe a person. Maybe a person can be defined by something he or she has done, or by some personality trait, or by a particular talent.

9. Encourage your child's autonomy. Give your child the freedom to make appropriate decisions, take appropriate risks, and foster a sense of competency. Let your child's own accomplishments give him a sense of worth and personal value.

10. Join a support group. Let your child know that he or she is not the only child in the world who was born with a craniofacial condition, and that others with the same condition are lovable, likable people as well. A support group will also give your child access to kindred spirits with whom he or she may discuss some of the issues that only another who has "been there" can truly understand.

With a good and healthy self image, your child can successfully turn the mirrors around. Then, instead of seeing himself as others see him, your child will look at others and reflect toward them how he sees himself.

The Tools We Give our Children

Our children who are cleft-affected, face life with a few more challenges than most other people -- and to meet those challenges, perhaps they need a few extra tools in their toolboxes. We have compiled here, a list of must-have tools that our children need if they are to be equipped for all that they will face as they go through life. Let us fill their toolbox from an early age and prepare them to be empowered individuals throughout life.

The tools for our children's work bench would include:

1) INFORMATION!!!!!!

How can they deal with any issue they know nothing about? Our children need to be given information in a form they can understand, and that means age-appropriate language. This is not the same as "age appropriate concepts", as a child is pretty capable of handling almost any information as long as it is presented in a way he or she understands it.

2) LANGUAGE

A child has to have the words to tell you how he or she feels inside. Many times, children fail to communicate a hurt simply because they don't know how to label it. My son's expression, "it hurt my heart" when a little girl in his preschool class made a comment about his lip was a good example. He groped for words to express to me how another child's words made him feel. What, though, if he didn't have the language to express that? Children recognize abstract concepts at a very early age, but it may take a while longer for them to develop language skills to label those concepts, unless we help them.

3) TRUST

A child must have someone in their lives that they can trust with their feelings and insecurities. If a parent always invalidates a child's words ("what do you mean nobody likes you??? EVERYBODY likes you - - now go on out and play!") then the child will not trust that parent with their deepest fears. Sometimes the hardest thing for a parent to do is to hear their child.

4) OUTLET

It's hard to bottle up unspent energy, and fear and anger are huge energy-generators. We need to allow our kids to cry, or to yell, or to find some way to release that energy in a way that will be healing to them. For some, it could be art. For others it could be acting. Still others may find an outlet in sports. Some may just need to yell for a bit. They need this chance to release, and sometimes we have to guide them toward a socially appropriate way to express it, yielding the most positive outcome.

5) ALTERNATIVE

Everybody is "best at" something -- even if it is only personal best. Our kids need positive alternatives on which to spend their energy. Our kids need to hear when we are proud of them -- they need to see the light spark in our eyes when we recognize a job well done. My daughter, Jessica, for instance cannot talk (apraxia) and she cannot write (poor fine motor - again, apraxia) but the day she brought her reader home to me and "read" it to me herself, she and I BOTH celebrated, and my girl felt like a million bucks. SHE DID GOOD!!!! and she knew it. Find your child's positives and never fail to point them out.

6) POSITIVE SELF-AWARENESS

Most people can point out what is WRONG with them, but how many of us feel comfortable identifying what is RIGHT? Our kids need to be able to counteract the negatives with known positives. We need to help our kids find their strengths - - not tell them their strengths -- help them find them. That way, when we are NOT there to point them out to them, our kids can still identify what is RIGHT and good about themselves.

Social Phobia, a natural outcome of a negative self-image, is definitely a dragon that we need to help our children slay early, while it is still nothing more than an annoying little lizard. With the proper tool of positive self-awareness, our children WON'T let it grow to a disabling condition!

7) SUPPORT SYSTEM/LOVE

So many things can be accomplished or endured in life if it is done in an atmosphere of unconditional love. The knowledge that someone loves and accepts you through it all makes you realize that you are worth loving. The single, most powerful thing we can do for our children is love them unconditionally. Love them simply because they are who they are. Never make them earn that love. It's a gift you are simply compelled to give. This is the refreshment in their arsenal of life. Give liberally, often, and with obvious pleasure! Make sure your child always knows that you represent a safe haven of support.

8) FOUNDATION (OPENNESS, HONESTY, LOVE)

Nurture, love, and support, your child. Talk honestly, welcome questions, and even welcome fears. Welcome these things with openness, love, and most of all HONESTY. Don't lie to your child. Nurture them and tell them the truth. No, it shouldn't matter what a person looks like on the outside, but in all honesty sometimes it does. And once in a while, the person for whom appearance matters appears, bringing with him all that ugliness. Only a foundation of openness, honesty and love will prepare your child for when that happens.

9) A MODEL OF EXPRESSION

Facts ARE one thing, but expression of emotion is another. You as parents have the responsibility to open up to your kids. When you are scared or angry, express that appropriately and in acceptable, productive ways. When they are scared or angry, encourage them to express it in the same appropriate, acceptable and productive ways. When they question, encourage that questioning. Be on the look out. If you don't open to it now, your child will face it later, often when they are on their own.

10) ADVOCACY

By first advocating for our child, we can teach them how to advocate for themselves. Particularly, we teach them that they have rights, and they have every right to claim them. Teach them by example how to effectively claim what is available to them. Help them to identify their own needs and then to identify ways to meet them.

11) CONTROL

Regardless of a child's developmental level, she should be allowed to exercise appropriate control in her situation. Very young children can choose what to take to the hospital, which parent will spend the night, what foods will be included in the liquid diet. Older kids can take more control. When will the surgery be scheduled? What sort of anesthesia will be used to go to sleep? Will she have this particular surgery at all? Involving our children in the decision making process gives them the tool of control.

12) REALISTIC EXPECTATIONS

Children need to know exactly what to expect and what not to expect from each procedure. Surgery leaves scars -- always. The child is born with a cleft, and later has a repaired cleft. It's not perfect, but it's completely acceptable. An expectation of perfection sets our children up for a sense of failure. One of the soundest and profoundest tools in a child's toolbox would be the tool of realistic expectations.

13)A Positive ATTITUDE

A positive attitude begets a positive attitude. And that, in turn, helps to ensure the best possible outcome. Negativism is a child's greatest foe, and a positive attitude is his greatest ally. Expect the best, and something good is likely to happen.

14) A PERSPECTIVE OF THE DE-VALUED CLEFT

Our children need to see the cleft as neither a good thing nor a bad thing - just a thing, a part of their lives. It is a part that will touch every area of their lives, but it is only ONE small part of the whole person. If the cleft is labeled a "bad thing" then your child will forever feel victimized. The reality is, cleft happens once in every 700 births, and your child pulled into the seven-hundredth slot. They neither won the lottery, nor did they draw the black dot. They simply were born with a birth condition that requires correction. That perspective will go a very long way in helping your child to handle questions and comments that may come their way concerning cleft issues.

15) COMMON EXPERIENCE

Knowing at least one other person who faces the same issues you face helps tremendously. You know you are not alone. Parents must seek out ways of making sure their child knows somebody else who was born with a cleft. Joining a support group with other cleft-affected individuals would help. Getting to know others via the internet and listservs such as cleft-talk helps. Letting them know persons of celebrity status (Jesse Jackson, Cheech Marin, Stacey Keach, and more.) who faced cleft issues helps too. It is so very lonely when you are the only one you know. And so refreshing when at last you meet another.

16) A SOCIAL OFFENSIVE

Help our children to be the one that others look up to - the one who has the good ideas - the one who initiates the fun activities. Teach our children to be PROactive in their social development, and not REactive - hoping that somebody notices them for all the right reasons.

17) VALIDATION

We need to validate for our children that their loss is real, and that they have a RIGHT to feel angry, sad, or even confused. They have, after all, suffered a valid loss. This loss can only find perspective once it is validated. To try to minimize it without first validating it would be similar to trying to stuff an air mattress back into its bag without first letting the air out. Acknowledge it so it can be released.

18) Permission

Our kids must have permission to feel what they feel; to express what is really going on inside of them, and not what they believe we want them to say. Teaching our children to "be calm, be still, be placid" is teaching them to bury their fears. And fears have a way of rising from the dead to be even MORE fearful later on. They have permission to be scared; Permission to be angry; Permission to express pain; And permission, also, to overcome those difficult emotions. They need to know that even if others do not understand their experience, they will at the very least accept it.

19) The Whole Person

A child is more than the sum of her/his body parts, and all of his/her parts are connected into one body/mind/spirit. This means, to cite only one example, that no matter how many times the parent hears the surgeon and other professionals say, when talking about their child, "revise THE lip, sculpt THE nose, lengthen THE columella," the parents take care to make it known that their utmost concern is the *whole* child. Communicating this respectful attitude to all individuals who will come in contact with the child -- from anesthesiologist to surgical team to recovery room nurse -- is essential. They must understand that they are dealing with a WHOLE little spiritual being in human form -- not just a collection of body parts -- and that they must behave accordingly.

So there you have it - - 19 tools in our children's tool chests. And it is up to us as parents to supply them. Are we up to the task? Well -- we'd better be. Our children, after all, cannot build without them.

Words of Encouragement
From those who know

The following individuals have grown up with a cleft. They were school children once. They know the importance of fitting in, and the angst of feeling different. But they have one thing school-aged kids and teens do not have. They have the benefit of perspective. They've been there. They've done that. They survived. In fact, looking back, they THRIVED! Hear now what they have to say.

Kelly
Unilateral cleft lip and palate – 30 yrs old
Australia

There are times in everyone's life (whether they are cleft affected or not) when other people might make them feel hurt or alone, just like Thumper the Bunny felt because he looked a little bit different. However, it is very important to know that these people really are few and far between (even though it sometimes doesn't feel that way). Try not to focus on these people, but instead put your energies into being a good, kind and generous person. This type of beauty shines through from the inside out and you will find yourself surrounded by people who see this and love you for being you, just the way you are.

Dana
Unilateral cleft lip and palate – 42 yrs old
Texas

Being born with a cleft lip and palate is a little bit different, but in a good way!

We can use our special smile to teach others that it's ok to have differences.

Our differences make us cool!

Some people are tall, some people are short. Some people have red hair or brown hair, some people have no hair!

If you ever feel bad about your cleft, it's ok! Talk to someone until you feel better. Just remember it's your smile that makes you strong!

Jacob
Unilateral cleft lip and palate (brother to Joey below) – 20 yrs. old
California

I was born with a cleft, but it was not a big deal for me. There are so many things in my life that are not about my being born with a cleft that sometimes I forget I even had a cleft. I'm proud to be a part of my family. I have a lot of good friends in my life. I work at a job that has meaning for me. Nobody makes a deal about my cleft. There are other things about me that people notice, like my skills, or my politics.

For me, in fact, the cleft brought good things to my life. I was adopted from Korea. If I didn't have a cleft, maybe I would not have come to my parents like I did. My mom says that's not so – that she would have adopted me anyway, but I wouldn't want to chance it.

Joey
Unilateral cleft lip and palate (and brother to Jacob, above) – 20 yrs old
California

I was born with what they call a very severe bilateral cleft. I didn't like having operations. That wasn't cool. But most of the time, I don't even think about my cleft. There are too many other things to think about in my life. Besides, what I found out growing up is, if the cleft is not a big deal to me, it won't be a big deal to anyone else either. I have some great friends that I wouldn't trade for all the world, and not one of them cares that I was born with a cleft.

Laura
Unilateral Cleft Lip and Palate - age 39
Texas

When I was about 4 years old, the 'experts' labeled me as "functionally retarded", which basically meant that I wasn't doing all the things a child my age should do. They put me in special education classes. I was teased a lot and that made it hard. It made me very defensive, with low self-esteem. Sometimes kids were nice and just had questions about what happened to give me a scar. They did not know what a cleft was and I didn't know anybody else with one. I did not mind answering them when they asked in a nice way. As I got older, I did have a hard time in school, but all I needed was a little extra help. By high school, I was no longer in special classes. I was even in an honors class with the "smart kids"! Girls, I did not date a lot in high school (that came later for me), but I did have a couple of boyfriends and a great social life. Just find something you love and get involved. The friends will come and they will not care if you have a cleft scar or not, they will like you for who you are. I went to college and got certified to be a respiratory technician and again for a teaching degree and now work at a preschool. Just give everything your best and you will succeed!

Sarah
Unilateral cleft lip and palate – 25 yrs old
Washington

Growing up with a cleft was, to say the least, a challenge. However, I am not saying having a cleft was bad in anyway. Without the experiences I have gained from this challenge I would not be the person I am today. Knowing the challenges that I faced as a child and teenager inspired me to work in the healthcare profession as a nurse. I am also an educator, which is a wonderful gift. I know how it feels to be in the hospital, I know how it feels to have surgery, these experiences are not specific to having a cleft and I am able to relate with my patients' experiences. Now I have a daughter with a cleft lip/palate and I plan on helping her through her challenges as well. Having a cleft is not something that should hold anyone back, it is a gift that you have and you should find your special way to share that gift with others!

David
Cleft palate – 54 yrs old
Illinois

I was born with a cleft palate in 1953 and had two surgeries when such operations were nowhere near as sophisticated as they are today. I went through the usual teasing as a child and the looks of not understanding what I say sometimes continue through today. However, my cleft has given me a *sui generis* sensitivity about the plight of all living things (including animals) that has profoundly shaped who I am. I graduated from UCLA Law in the 80's and have recently argued a case before the California Supreme Court. In addition, I am a co-author of the biography, *You Send Me, The LIfe and Times of Sam Cooke,* published in 1994 by William Morrow (with a baseball bio due out in 2009) . When I am not practicing law or involved in a literary project, I am a reference law librarian at a public library. With half my life behind me, my only concern is that I will run out of time to fulfill all of my dreams. I can assure you I would not have accomplished one tenth of my achievements if I had been born ordinary -- without a cleft.

Jan
Unilateral right-side cleft lip – age 52
Michigan

Today, at the age of 52 I am a confident, compassion woman because of my cleft. I love deeply; live fully with compassion and understanding for all who were not born perfect. I appreciate all that I have including my cleft and I thank God for this defect because it has made me the woman I am. Don't ever be ashamed of your scar. Talk about it, share your experiences with friends and family. Even learn to add humor as you face the surgeries and know that God is with you every step of the way. Lastly, when someone treats you mean and yes, cruel because you have a small defect, they are someone you need to just love and treat with compassion.

Brian
Unilateral cleft lip and palate – age 46
London

Keep you head up and keep smiling - you don't look as different as you think you do. When people say they didn't even notice that you had a cleft lip - believe them - it's the truth!"

Cody
Unilateral Cleft Lip and Palate – Age 46
Minnesota

You will succeed—heck; you've learned more things about human nature and how to relate to people than folks twice your age. As crazy as it may sound, having a cleft has empowered you. The key is to always utilize, and focus on, your strengths. Being born with a cleft has enabled you to listen closer than others; to consider what people say and do so with a deep understanding of their perspective; to overcome challenges; to know the right way to handle most any circumstance; and much more. An argument can be made that you're lucky to have a cleft—I know, hard to believe, but the argument can be made.

The challenges you face can, and will be overcome—they will build your character and make you a stronger person. Your "difference" or "differences" will make you more resilient and more optimistic than people who are not faced with such challenges. I'm not feeding you a line. I know it can be extremely tough sometimes—but those times are temporary. I graduated valedictorian of my high school, earned scholarships to attend a premier business school, and am now the Chief Financial Officer of a corporation. Bottom line, you can and will do whatever you want because you've all ready overcame more than most everyone your age. Best wishes and I look forward to rea**ding your success stories!**

Kara
Bilateral Cleft Lip and Palate – 28 yrs old
Massachusetts

One thing got me through the difficult times: hope. Thumper had hope, too. He dreamed about being accepted. In time it happened. In the same way, the right people did enter my life and accept me. I always held out hope that things would get better. With time, things did get better. I thank my parents for giving me this hope. They were always very helpful and loving. They told me things would be okay and made sure that I kept trying to make new friends. I still hold that hope inside me today, knowing that every day is an opportunity for someone or some thing positive to come into my life.

Other Books by Author, Joanne Green
Available at sagabooks.net

The Story of Lippy the Lion

A prince is born! But this prince is born with a cleft lip. This story tells of the emotional drama that plays out in the heart of the parents who would rather change the world than subject their child to the surgery that is necessary to level the playing field for this beautiful child. Mommy Lion must learn, and learn quickly, that reconstructive surgery is something she does for, and not to, her child.

To My Child, Concerning Your Birthmother

Adopted children know they are loved by their parents, but the question often nags – how could my birthmother give me away? This book helps the child to peek into the mind and the heard of the woman who gave her life. A poignant poem written by an adoptive mother who never wanted her son to feel unloved or unwanted by anyone.

American Hero

Who are our American Heroes? Certainly the men and woman who faithfully serve our country through the armed forces are heroes, but so also are those they leave at home while deployed. American Hero looks at a day in the life of both a little boy and the father he shares with the nation through deployment.

About the Author

Joanne Green is the founding director of Wide Smiles (www.widesmiles.org), an information and networking program for individuals and families dealing with cleft lip and palate. She is the mother of three children who were born with clefts. Jacob was born with a complete unilateral cleft lip and palate. Joey and Jessica were born with complete bilateral cleft lips and palates. All three of her children joined her family as babies by way of adoption.

Joanne is also the list owner of a cleft-talk, a listserv for families who deal with cleft and craniofacial issues. To subscribe to that list, send an email to majordomo@bmtmicro.com and put "subscribe cleft_talk2" in the message field of your email.

Joanne lives with her family in Stockton, California. She is a sixth grade language arts and social studies teacher in the public schools, as well as Wide Smiles director. In her spare time, she writes.

About the illustrator

Penny Tennant is the mother of three children: Kate Phillip and Andrew. When her oldest child, Andrew, was born with a cleft palate in late 1995, Wide Smiles and Cleft-Talk were a valuable source of information and support.

Penny lives in New Mexico with her family. She is a technical illustrator for Weidlinger Associates Inc. In her "spare time," she is the editor of the New Mexico Autism Society Newsletter and is active in PTA, Scouting and Taekwondo.

The illustrations were originally drawn in pencil and colorized on the computer for the Wide Smiles' website. For this book they were rescanned and colorized and enhanced with photos from her New Mexico garden.

LaVergne, TN USA
30 September 2009
159420LV00002BA